A Connecticut Yankee in King Arthur's Court

by
Mark Twain

adapted by
Lucia Monfried

MOBY BOOKS

PLAYMORE, INC. Publishers
Under arrangement with I. WALDMAN & SON, INC.
New York, New York

CONTENTS

About the Author

Mark Twain, one of America's greatest and most beloved writers, was born Samuel Langhorne Clemens in 1835. He spent his boyhood in Hannibal, Missouri, a town on the Mississippi. He used his boyhood experiences in this town in two of his greatest novels, *The Adventures of Tom Sawyer* and *The Adventures of Huckleberry Finn.*

Samuel Clemens left Hannibal and worked as a Mississippi river pilot, a prospector, and then a journalist. He took the pen name, Mark Twain, and traveled all over America and Europe. His books on his travels made him famous, and he married well and settled in Hartford, Connecticut.

He was a man of many talents. He was energetic and hot-tempered, and known for his outspoken opinions as well as his humor. Toward the end of his life, he suffered many misfortunes. He lost all his money and was forced to make lecture tours around the world. He made people laugh, but behind much of this laughter was bitterness and sorrow. Mark Twain died outside of Hartford in 1910.

Characters You Will Meet

Hank Morgan, *the Connecticut Yankee*
Clarence, *a page who becomes Hank's right-
    hand man*
King Arthur, *King of England*
Merlin, *the king's magician*
Knights of the Round Table
    Sir Launcelot
    Sir Dinidan
    Sir Sagramour
Queen Guenever, *King Arthur's wife*
Alisande, *a pretty girl with a taste for
    adventure*
Morgan Le Fay, *an evil queen*
A sick woman
An old abbot at the Valley of Holiness
Marco, *the coal burner*
Dowley, *the blacksmith*
A slave master

The Curious Stranger

Chapter 1
The Stranger's History

A curious stranger appeared one day at Warwick Castle in England. He carried a large old book, yellowed with age, and talked of Sir Launcelot, Sir Galahad and all the other great names of the Round Table. He himself looked ancient, and when he talked, he seemed to drift away into some other time.

He knew all about those olden times. He said he had been there and seen it all. His marvelous story was written down in the book. The first page began this way:

I am an American. I was born and reared

in Hartford, in the state of Connecticut. So I am a Yankee. I learned my real trade in the great arms factory there. I learned to make everything—guns, revolvers, cannon, boilers, engines, all the machinery there was. I could make anything anybody wanted—anything in the world. If I couldn't make a thing, I could invent one.

I was head superintendent, with more than a thousand men under me. They were rough, and I had my share of fights. At last I met my match. I got smashed in the head with a crowbar. It knocked me out, but I didn't feel a thing. The world went out in darkness.

When I came to again, I was sitting under an oak tree in a broad country landscape. There was a fellow looking at me—a fellow fresh out of a picture book. He was in old time armor, with a helmet on his head, and he had a shield, a sword, and a long spear. His horse had on armor, too, and silk

Waking Up in a Country Landscape

trappings that hung to the ground.

"Fair sir, will ye fight?" said this fellow.

"Will I which?" I said. "Get along back to your circus or I'll report you."

But then this man came rushing at me with his spear pointed straight ahead. I saw he meant business, and I was up the tree when he arrived. He then said I was his property, and since he had his spear and I had nothing, I agreed to go with him.

We marched along, but we didn't come to any circus, so I gave up that idea. I asked him how far we were from Hartford, but he said he never had heard of the place.

At the end of an hour we saw a town, and beyond on a hill, a huge gray fortress with towers and turrets.

"Hartford?" said I, pointing.

"Camelot," said he.

"Camelot," Said He.

The Girl Is Startled.

Chapter 2
Camelot

"Camelot—Camelot," said I to myself. "I don't remember hearing of it before."

The landscape was lovely, full of the smell of flowers and twittering of birds. The road was a narrow, winding path with hoofprints in it.

Presently a young girl came along. She paid no attention to the circus man, as if she saw men like him every day. But when she noticed me, then there was a change. Up went her hands, and her mouth dropped open. I couldn't understand why she should be startled at me and not at the other man.

There were cabins with thatched roofs, surrounded with garden patches. There were people too. The men had long uncombed hair, and the women wore robes that came below the knee. All of these people stared at me and ran in to get their families. But nobody ever noticed that other fellow.

Presently there was a distant blare of military music. A cavalcade came into view, glorious with helmets and banners. We followed along with it, climbing until we reached the huge castle. There was an exchange of bugle blasts. The gates were flung open, the drawbridge lowered. We followed into a great paved court, with towers and turrets on all sides.

There was much greeting and running, and a gay display of color, noise and confusion.

A Gay Display of Color and Noise

Hank Wants to Know Where He Is.

Chapter 3
King Arthur's Court

The moment I got a chance, I stepped aside and touched a common-looking man on the shoulder. "Friend," I said, "do me a kindness. Do you belong to this asylum or are you just visiting?"

He looked me over stupidly and said, "Fair sir, me seemeth—"

"That will do," I said. "You talk like the rest and I know you are a patient."

I moved away, keeping my eye out for any chance person that might come along who could tell me where I was. A handsome boy was coming towards me. He wore tights and a plumed satin cap. He said he was a page and began to talk and laugh in a boyish fashion until I stopped him. He had just said that he was born in the year 513!

It made the cold chills creep over me. "Maybe I didn't hear you right," I said. "Say it again. What year was that?"

"Five thirteen."

"Come, my boy, be honest. Are you in your right mind?" I asked.

He said he was.

"And this isn't an asylum, where they cure crazy people?" I asked.

He said it wasn't.

"Well, then," I said, "either I am a lunatic or something just as awful has happened. Now tell me, honest and true, where am I?"

"In King Arthur's Court," he answered.

"And what year is it now?"

"Five twenty-eight—twentieth of June," he

A Boy Born in the Year 513?

said.

I felt a sinking at my heart, but I seemed to believe the boy. I don't know why. Everything in me said they were all lunatics, that this couldn't be true. I had been knocked in the head in the nineteenth century to wake up in the sixth!

But at that moment I did remember that a total eclipse of the sun occurred on the twenty-first of June in the year 528. An eclipse of the sun happens when the moon moves in front of the sun and blots out its light in the middle of the day. That eclipse had occurred at twelve noon. The twenty-first was tomorrow! If I could wait till then, I'd know whether the boy was telling the truth.

Then, being a practical Connecticut man, I turned all my attention to my situation of the moment.

"Now Clarence, my boy, if I may call you that," I said to the page, "who is that knight

A Total Eclipse of the Sun

who brought me here?"

"That is the good knight and lord, Sir Kay," he said. He also said that I was Sir Kay's prisoner, and that I would be flung into a dungeon until my friends rescued me— unless I chanced to rot first. After dinner Sir Kay would exhibit me before King Arthur and the Round Table. He would brag about capturing me, and then I would be thrown into the dungeon.

"But I'll find a way to come and see you and help get word to your friends," Clarence said.

Get word to my friends! I thanked him. I couldn't do less. And then it was time for me to be led in.

Time to Be Led In

Knights Sitting at the Round Table

Chapter 4
Knights of the Round Table

Well, it was a curious kind of spectacle. The room was very lofty and hung with banners. The floor was of big stones and the walls were covered with hangings.

In the middle was a huge oak table which they called the Round Table. Around it sat a great company of men dressed in splendid colors. They were drinking from ox horns and gnawing bones, which they then threw to the dogs.

I looked around at the manly faces of the Knights of the Round Table. The king was noble, Sir Galahad, pure. There was majesty and greatness in Sir Launcelot of the Lake.

A very old and white-bearded man in a flowing black gown rose, swaying his ancient head.

"Who is it?" I asked the boy.

"Merlin, the mighty liar and magician. Men fear him, for they think he has storms and lightning and devils at his call."

Next Sir Dinidan stood and told a joke. The boy didn't laugh. He said most of Sir Dinidan's jokes were rotten.

Then Sir Kay rose. He told how he had found me in a far land of wild men who all wore the same silly clothes I did—clothes that were enchanted. He said he'd killed my thirteen knights, but had spared my life so he could show me to the king and court.

He ended by condemning me to die at noon on the twenty-first.

Merlin, the Mighty Magician and Liar

Hank Thinks He Has Dreamed It All.

Chapter 5
An Inspiration

After this I was carried off. I was shoved into a dark and narrow cell with some moldy straw for a bed and rats for company.

I was so tired even my fear couldn't keep me awake. When I did awake, I thought, "What an astonishing dream I've had."

But then I heard the sound of rusty chains, and Clarence stood before me.

"Are you still here?" I said. "Go along with the rest of the dream."

"Pray, what dream?" he asked.

"The dream I am in Arthur's Court."

"Oh, la, indeed," he laughed. "And is it a dream that you're to be burned tomorrow? Ho-ho, answer me that."

My situation was distressing. Being burned to death, even in a dream, was a thing to be avoided at any cost.

"Ah, Clarence," I sighed, "the only friend I've got. Don't fail me. Help me to devise some way of escaping this place."

"Escape?" he said. "One may not hope to escape." The boy began to tremble. "I do not want to tell you, but—"

"Come, come, be brave. Speak out."

He whispered, "Merlin has woven a spell around this dungeon, and there is not a man in these kingdoms who would try to cross the lines with you."

"Merlin has wrought a spell," I laughed. "Merlin, that cheap old humbug. Bosh, pure bosh!"

Clarence had fallen to his knees.

Clarence Fears Merlin's Power.

"Oh, beware," he said, "these are awful words. Any moment these walls may crumble upon us if you say such things."

Now Clarence's fright gave me a good idea. If everybody was so afraid of Merlin's pretended magic, certainly a man like me should be able to make the most of such a state of things. I said:

"Get up, lad. Do you know why I laughed? I'll tell you. Because I'm a magician too.

"Now look here, Clarence. I'm your friend, right? I want you to do me a favor. Get word to the king that I am the grand muck-a-muck magician myself. And I am arranging a little disaster if any harm comes to me."

The poor boy was in such a state he could hardly answer. But he promised everything.

You see, it was then I had the inspiration. I would use the eclipse. I remembered how Columbus or Cortez had used an eclipse to frighten savages. I could use it myself.

"I'm a Magician Too."

Clarence came back and said:

"I brought your message to the king, and he was frightened. But Merlin said that you are mad. He said your threat is foolishness. He said that you must say what your great disaster is."

I was silent for a moment. Then I said:

"Tell the king that at noon tomorrow—the hour I am to be burned—I will smother the world in darkness. I will blot out the sun, and it shall never shine again!"

"I Will Blot Out the Sun!"

The Stake Is Ready.

Chapter 6
The Eclipse

When I thought of the eclipse, I was as happy as could be. It would be sure to save me. But not only that. It would be the making of me.

The morning came. I heard footsteps. The door opened and a guard said to me, "The stake is ready. Come. Haste thee."

They took hold of me and pulled me through the maze of underground corridors to the courtyard. There was the stake, and on all sides sat the multitudes.

As I was being chained to the stake, the

crowd was silent. Dread was in their faces. A man knelt to light the fire. A monk began some words in Latin, but stopped suddenly and raised his eyes toward the sky.

The multitude rose slowly and stared into the sky. I followed their eyes. As sure as guns, there was my eclipse beginning! I struck a grand pose, my arm pointing to the sun and said:

"Stay where you are. If any man moves— even the king—I will blast him with thunder and strike him with lightning."

The multitude sank meekly to their seats. I knew I was master of the situation now.

"Name any terms," the king shouted, "but banish this disaster! Spare the sun! Look, it grows darker."

So, this *was* the sixth century, and not a dream. Yes, I *was* in King Arthur's Court. I decided then to make the most of it. I tried to remember how long a total eclipse lasts. I

Hank's Eclipse Begins.

wanted my timing to be right.

"These are the terms. You shall appoint me your chief minister forever," I called.

The king's voice rose:

"Away with his bonds. Bow down to him, high and low, for he is the king's minister."

I then asked for clothes, for my modern ones would never do.

Clothes were brought. It grew darker and darker while I struggled with those awkward sixth-century clothes. It got to be pitch dark and the crowd groaned with horror. At last the eclipse was total.

Then I lifted my hands and said:

"Let the enchantment dissolve."

First there was a hush. But when the rim of the sun showed, the crowd broke loose and came pouring down with blessings and gratitude.

Struggling with the Clothes

The People Come to See Hank.

Chapter 7
Merlin's Tower

I was now the second most important person in the kingdom. Much was made of me. I had servants and new clothes and everything I wished.

One thing troubled me at first. The people took a great interest in me. It turned out that the eclipse had scared the British world almost to death, and people came from miles around to see me. I had to go out a dozen times a day and show myself. This, of course, turned Merlin green with envy and spite.

The multitudes presently wanted another

miracle. They wanted to say they had seen a miracle themselves. So I thought out a plan. I gave public notice that in two weeks time I would blow up Merlin's stone tower by fires from heaven.

I took Clarence into my confidence and told him this was the sort of miracle which required a little preparation. Secretly, we made a few bushels of first-rate blasting powder and constructed a lightning rod.

Working by night we stowed the powder in the tower. On the thirteenth night we put our lightning rod up right in the blasting powder.

In order to work this miracle, I needed a stormy night with lots of lightning flashes. When the lightning struck the rod, the rod would send a charge down to the powder, and it would explode.

By the evening, the storm I was waiting for was near. I called Merlin:

Stowing the Blasting Powder in the Tower

"It is only fair to give you a chance to break my enchantments." He burnt a pinch of powder and began to make passes in the air.

By now the lightning was flashing, so I said, "You have had time enough." I made three passes in the air, and then there was an awful crash. The tower leaped into the sky in chunks along with a fountain of fire.

It was an effective miracle. The king wanted to banish Merlin, but I said no. I thought he would be useful to work the weather, and I even had his tower rebuilt. But he was not grateful. He never even said thank you.

Hank's Second Miracle!

A Quaint and Simple Race

Chapter 8
The Boss

The tower miracle made me even more powerful. My power was very large. Yes, in power, I was equal to the king. At the same time, there was another power that was a little stronger than both of us put together. That was the Church.

It was a curious country, but I was getting used to it. And the people! They were a quaint and simple race. Truth be it, most of King Arthur's British nation were slaves and wore the iron collar on their necks. The rest called themselves freemen. But they really gave their all for King and Church.

I was admired and feared, but I was not royalty. And those people had more respect for royalty and nobility than for brains and talent.

I could have got a title easily. But I didn't ask for it. I couldn't have felt fine and proud about any title except one that should come from the nation itself.

In the course of years, I did win one. It fell from the lips of a blacksmith, and I liked it. It later became as familiar as the king's name. I was never known by any other name afterward. This title, in modern speech, was THE BOSS.

The Boss

A Tournament

Chapter 9
The Tournament

They were always having grand tournaments at Camelot. The knights came from the ends of the country, and they brought their ladies and squires too. These tournaments were grand and stirring events.

There was one every week and I always attended. Every now and then, Launcelot and the knights urged me to enter. I said I would, by and by, but that there were too many government matters for me to look after at the time.

One day when I was watching the tournament, Sir Dinidan came and told me a terrible joke. As he was leaving, I groaned, "Oh, that was awful!" Sir Sagramour, who had just jousted his opponent on the field, caught my remark. He thought I was speaking about his performance.

Well, he felt he had to right that insult, and he challenged me to a joust. Whenever one of those people got a thing in his head, there was no changing it. So I didn't even try to explain what I really had meant.

Sir Sagramour then named the day we would settle the score. It was three or four years in the future, but I said I would be ready.

Sir Sagramour Challenges Hank.

The Brightest Men Hank Could Find

Chapter 10
Beginnings of Civilization

The Round Table heard of the challenge. The king thought I should set forth in quest of adventures so that I would be more worthy to meet Sir Sagramour.

I was pretty well pleased with what I had done in the kingdom and thought I could afford to leave. In various nooks and corners I had the beginnings of all sorts of industries underway. I gathered the brightest minds I could find and trained them in my man factories—secretly, of course.

The people didn't know it, but I had the

civilization of the nineteenth century blooming under their very noses. I had schools and shops. Everything was being put on a scientific basis.

Clarence was twenty-two now, and he was my chief assistant, my right-hand man. There was nothing he could not do.

Our greatest project was setting up a telegraph and telephone. We had a gang of men striking across the country stringing ground wires and connecting towns, all at night.

Other than that, the general condition of the country was the way I had found it.

Four years had passed in this way, and lately the king had been reminding me that I ought to be starting out on my adventures. I was expecting this break, so I made ready to leave.

Hank's Right-Hand Man

The Girl with the Story

Chapter 11
The Yankee in Search of Adventures

There was never such a country for wandering liars. Hardly a month went by without someone arriving at the castle with a tale about some princess being held in captivity in some faraway castle. And everyone believed these stories.

One day, a girl arrived with a story. She said her mistress was locked in a castle with forty-four young and beautiful girls. Three ogres guarded them. Was there a knight who would rescue them? Every knight jumped for this opportunity for adventure, but the king said I would go and free the princesses.

I sent for the girl, intending to ask her a few questions. She was pretty, but the only thing I got from the conversation was her name. It was Alisande.

When Clarence came back, he said he had been wondering what I had wanted to ask the girl. I said:

"Don't I want to find the castle? How else would I go about it?"

"She will go with you. They always do."

"Ride with me? Nonsense!" I said.

"But of course she will," he said. "You will see." And it was true.

Everyone was talking about my journey. We were to start at dawn, for that was the usual way. But I had a difficult time with my armor. It was so troublesome to get into.

The sun was just up, and the king and court were all on hand to see us off. I had to be carried to my horse and helped up. They

Starting Off at Dawn

fixed my feet in the stirrups and handed me a spear. And so we started.

It was lovely and pleasant in the cool early morning, but a couple of hours after sunup it wasn't as pleasant as it had been. The sun beat down and warmed up my iron suit more and more. I got Alisande to take off my helmet, and she filled it with water which she poured down inside the armor until I was soaked and comfortable. I brought my pipe, and I was wishing I could have a smoke. But I could not light it. I had forgotten matches.

Night approached, and we camped. But we were off before sunrise, Alisande riding and I limping along behind.

We came upon a group of ragged men mending the road. They were overwhelmed when I proposed to have breakfast with them. Knights in armor did not usually mix with such lowly people. They gave me a flint and steel, and helped me onto my horse. I lit my

Cooling Water

pipe. The first blast of smoke that shot through the bars of my helmet made those people run for the woods. They thought I was a fire-belching dragon. I told them to come back, and I finally convinced them that this was only a little bit of enchantment that would work no harm. With their fears gone, they were so full of wonder at my fireworks that I had to smoke a couple of pipes before they would let me go. But I had learned something that might come in useful if I was in a dangerous situation.

And I did use this trick the next afternoon. Sandy—for that is what I called Alisande now—was radiant with the effect it had.

A Fire-Belching Dragon?

Morgan Le Fay

Chapter 12
Morgan Le Fay

That night we approached a large castle which stood on high ground. This castle belonged to Morgan Le Fay, sister of King Arthur and wife of King Uriens. I have nothing pleasant to tell about the visit.

I had heard stories about Morgan Le Fay, and I wasn't expecting anything pleasant. All her ways were wicked; all her history was black with crime.

As soon as we were within the castle gates, we were ordered into her presence. To my surprise, she was beautiful.

Presently, a handsome young page came with something on a tray. Kneeling to present it to her, he lost his balance and fell against her knee. She slipped a knife into him and he fell dead. Servants were called to remove the body, and all the while, Morgan Le Fay was talking sweetly to us. Sandy and I were aghast.

In the midst of the talk, I said something good about King Arthur, forgetting for the moment how this woman hated her brother. She called for her guards:

"Take this rascal to the dungeons!"

As a guard laid hands on me, Sandy piped up and said:

"Do you want destruction on yourself? It is the Boss!"

The guard froze. Morgan Le Fay smiled, but she was not able to cover up her fright.

We had dinner in the great banqueting hall, and everything was as fine and lavish

"Take This Rascal to the Dungeons!"

as could be. By midnight everyone was tired and sore from laughing.

Suddenly, at the bottom of the hall there appeared an old woman leaning upon a stick. She pointed the stick at the queen and cried out:

"The curse of God upon you, woman without pity! You have slain my grandchild, my only comfort in this world."

The queen rose up with the death light in her eye:

"Lay hands on her. To the stake with her!"

Sandy gave me a look. She was up and facing the queen. "Madame," she said, pointing at me, "*he* says this may not be. Recall the commandment, or he will dissolve the castle and it shall vanish."

It was some promise! But the queen did not resist and did as Sandy said. Then the people in the hall rose and rushed for the door before I could change my mind and puff the

Sandy Stands Up to the Queen.

castle into space.

I had had enough of this grisly place by now. But there was something I wanted to do before leaving. I told the queen I had been freeing all the prisoners from the jails at Camelot and neighboring castles. I asked her permission to see her prisons. She finally consented, and we went down under the castle's foundations where there were many cells cut out of the rock.

There were forty-seven prisoners in those awful ratholes. And dear me, most of them were in there for small crimes, or no crimes at all. The newest prisoner's crime was a remark he had made. He said he believed that underneath, men were all alike. And for this they had put him in prison. I set him loose and sent him to my man factory.

There were five captives whose names and crimes were no longer known. They themselves had forgotten the details. All of them

Morgan Le Fay's Prisons

had been in prison for thirty-five years. The king and queen knew nothing about them.

I said to Morgan Le Fay, "Then why in the world didn't you set them free?"

The question puzzled her. It had never come up in her mind.

Well, she was a curious one, Morgan Le Fay. I could barely wait till we were on the road again.

A Curious One

Sandy Sees the "Castle."

Chapter 13
The Ogre's Castle

We were on the road two days when Sandy began to show signs of excitement. She said we were approaching the ogre's castle. My heart began to thump. This statement reminded me I had almost forgotten our quest.

Presently, Sandy slid from her horse, motioned me to stop, and went creeping toward a row of bushes. She said in a whisper, "Look, the castle looms ahead."

"A castle?" I asked. "It is nothing but a pigsty."

She didn't understand and said thoughtfully, "A pigsty? Well, it must be enchanted now, although it was not enchanted before. How strange that to me it appears as a castle, and to you a pigsty."

I didn't understand how she could think a pigsty was a castle, but I knew I wouldn't be able to argue her out of her delusion. So I went along with it. "It is only *my* eyes that are under the enchantment. Only to *me* does the castle appear as a pigsty and the princesses I came to rescue as hogs. They remain princesses to themselves and to you And I suppose those swineherds, the men who are tending the hogs, are the ogres."

"Oh, are *they* changed also?"

I shook my head in amazement. "Don't you be afraid," I told her. "I will make short work of this."

I left Sandy there and struck up a trade with the swineherds. I bought out all the hogs for sixteen pennies.

The Enchanted "Ogres"

When I opened the sty gate, Sandy fell upon those hogs with tears of joy running down her cheeks. She greeted them and called them by names fit for princesses.

I thought about Sandy's curious delusion. Here she was, as sane as could be, and she, like everyone else around her, believed in enchantments. If I told Sandy that I had seen a wagon spin along at fifty miles an hour and had listened to someone talk who was hundreds of miles away, she would have thought I was crazy.

If I was to be sane in this world, I knew to keep my stories about locomotives and telephones to myself. I also knew the world was round, but as I was the only person in the kingdom with this opinion, I recognized it was wise to keep quiet about this matter too.

The next morning I said, "Well then, Sandy, we have been successful on our adventure. I have rescued the 'princesses.' I

Sandy's Curious Delusion

will go home and report."

"I also am ready," she said. "I will go with you, and I will not part from you until some champion shall fairly win me."

Hank Keeps His Stories to Himself.

A Procession of Pilgrims

Chapter 14
The Pilgrims

The first thing we struck that day was a procession of pilgrims. It was a pleasant, friendly, merry group. Sandy said they were going to the Valley of Holiness to drink the miraculous waters and be cleansed from sin.

"Where is this watering place?" I asked.

"A two-day journey from here" was her answer. "It is a celebrated place," she continued. "In olden times an abbot and his monks lived there. None were more holy than they. But there was always a lack of water there. The holy abbot prayed, and a great stream of water burst forth.

"Now that they had water, the monks begged and begged their abbot to build a bath. So he did. The monks entered the bath and came out washed as white as snow. But this bath must have displeased God, for the waters stopped flowing. All prayers were in vain. So the abbot destroyed the bath. The waters gushed forth again, and they have flowed unto this day. The fame of this miracle has spread far and wide."

We joined the pilgrims and rode all day. When I rose next morning, a knight came riding. I ran to greet him, and he said he was coming from the Valley of Holiness.

"Sir, it is bad news I bring. Are these pilgrims? Then gather and hear my tale, for what ye seek, ye seek in vain. A misfortune has struck the valley—the same misfortune that happened long ago!"

"The miraculous fountain has ceased to flow!" the pilgrims shouted together.

A Knight with Bad News

"The fountain has been dry nine days now," he explained. "Prayers began and holy processions. At last they sent for you, Sir Boss, to try magic and enchantment. And if you could not come, the messenger was to fetch Merlin. He has been there three days now, but he has not started a whiff of moisture yet."

After breakfast, I wrote this note:

CHEMICAL DEPARTMENT: SEND TWO OF NO. 1 AND SIX OF NO. 4, WITH DETAILS. SEND TWO OF MY TRAINED ASSISTANTS.

I gave the note to the knight and said, "Go to Camelot as fast as you can fly, brave knight, and show the writing to Clarence."

"I will, Sir Boss," he said and he was off.

A Note for Clarence

The Old Abbot Is Overjoyed.

Chapter 15
The Holy Fountain

The pilgrims decided to continue, and before sunset we stood at the Valley of Holiness. The scene was mournful. The bells tolled softly and sadly.

The old abbot was overjoyed to see me.

"Do not delay, my son," he said. "Get to your work." But I told him I could not work until Merlin finished.

He begged. I refused. Of course, it would have been best for Merlin to quit right then, since he would never be able to start the water with his kind of magic. Merlin was trying awfully hard, and I did not want him to retire until I was ready. I would not be ready until I got my things from Camelot, and that would take two or three days.

Matters were about as I expected. The "fountain" was an ordinary well. It had been dug and stoned up in the ordinary way.

The well was in a chamber in the center of the chapel. When there was water, it was drawn up by monks and poured into stone channels which flowed out through the chapel.

I had an idea the well had sprung a leak, that some of the stones near the bottom had fallen out and the water was escaping out through small cracks. I entered the well chamber, called in some monks, and locked the door. I took a candle and made them lower me down the well in the bucket. I was right. A large section of the wall was gone, and there was a good, big crack. There was

Down the Well

water below that level—the bucket just did not reach that deep.

Here they were praying and tolling their bells, and no one had thought to drop a fishline down the well or go down in it and find out what was really the matter.

The problem was simple to solve, but I said to the monks after I came up, "It is a difficult miracle to restore water in a dry well. But we will try, if Brother Merlin fails. I can do this miracle, and I shall. But it will tax my powers."

As a matter of business it was good to get the idea around that it was difficult.

Hank Reassures the Monks.

Panting and Exhausted

Chapter 16
The Miracle of the Fountain

On Saturday noon I went to the well and looked on awhile. Merlin was still burning smoke powders and muttering gibberish. At the end of twenty minutes he dropped down, panting and exhausted, and said:

"There is no man who can break the spell. The water will flow no more. I have done what man could."

The abbot turned to me. "You have heard him. Is it true?"

"There are conditions under which the spell can be broken," I answered.

"What are the conditions?" inquired the abbot. "We will grant them."

"Oh, nothing difficult," I said. "I want the well and the surroundings entirely to myself from sunset today until I remove the ban."

My experts arrived in the evening. They had brought everything I needed—tools, pump, fireworks—for a good miracle.

My boys were experts in all sorts of things, and an hour before sunrise we had the leak mended. The water began to rise. Within nine hours it had risen to its usual level.

We put in a little iron pump—one of the first turned out by my works—and ran a lead pipe to the floor of the chapel, so the crowds outside could see the gushing water.

We put rockets and fireworks on the roof of the chapel and built a platform about two hundred yards off for the abbot. When you are going to do a miracle, you want to do it right. You can't throw in too much style.

Experts in All Sorts of Things

The news of the disaster to the well had traveled far. People had been pouring into the valley. I decided to stage the miracle on Sunday night, and criers went round early on Sunday evening and announced the coming event.

I was at the platform at ten-thirty when the abbot's procession arrived. Merlin came along with the abbot. The multitudes were already waiting.

I stood on the platform. I knew the boys were at the pump now, ready to turn the water on. So I said to the abbot:

"The time is come, Father. I am about to command the spell to dissolve."

Then I shouted to the people:

"Behold! In another minute the spell will be broken, and you will see water gush from the chapel door."

Then I touched off the rockets, and they burst into a storm of flashing jewels in mid-

Hank Breaks the Spell.

sky. A cry of joy broke from the people, for there in the glare they saw the water leaping forth. The abbot could not speak a word, but enfolded me in his arms. The people threw themselves down in the water and kissed it.

When I started back to the chapel the people fell back. I taught some of the monks how to use the pump. To the monks the pump was a miracle itself. Everyone was full of wonder and admiration.

It had been a great night.

The Water Gushes Again!

A Cave with a Surprise

Chapter 17
The Telephone Line

We achieved great success in the Valley of Holiness. I even persuaded them to open up the old bath. Another triumph!

I had made up my mind to go out into the countryside alone, leaving Sandy behind to rest up. My idea was to disguise myself as a peasant freeman and wander through the country. This would give me a chance to eat and stay with the lowliest of free citizens on equal terms. In this way I would learn about their everyday life.

One morning, on a long walk, I came upon a cave and looked in. My surprise was great.

Back in the gloom I heard the click of a little bell, followed by, "Hello, hello! Is this you, Camelot?"

How fantastic! Here in this valley of the miracle was the real miracle—a cave turned into a telephone office.

I recognized the telephone clerk as one of my boys. He said wires were being laid by night, and this office had just opened.

He called Camelot for me, and Clarence was sent for. It was good to hear his voice again.

"What's new?" I asked.

"King Arthur and the queen do start now for the Valley of Holiness to pay homage to the waters and cleanse themselves of sin," was his reply.

Calling Camelot

Disguised as Peasants

Chapter 18
The Yankee and the King Travel Disguised

When the king and queen arrived, I told the king I was going out disguised as a freeman to get to know the people. He was all afire with the idea and wanted to go too.

I thought he ought to tell the queen. He looked sad and said mournfully:

"You forget that Launcelot is here. Guenever does not notice me when he is near."

That was true, and everyone knew it.

Later, I took the king to my private quarters to cut his hair and help him get the hang of the lowly clothes he had to wear

We slipped away at dawn and stopped to rest later so I could look for water. I saw some noble people coming into view and ran back.

"Pardon, my king, but jump! Jump to your feet. Some nobility are coming."

"Is that a marvel?" he asked, forgetting entirely. "Let them come."

"But my liege, you must not be seen sitting. Rise—but stand humbly. You are a peasant, you know," I reminded him.

"True," he said, "I had forgot."

"A humbler attitude, my king," I hissed. "Duck your head more—still more—droop it!"

He did his best, but that was the most you could say for it. He just could not look humble. And he was always frightening me. On the second day he pulled out a knife from inside his robe, saying he thought he should carry a weapon for protection.

"But people of our condition are not

Standing Humbly Before a Knight

allowed to carry arms," I explained. "What would a lord say if he caught a peasant with a daggar?" So he threw it away.

Every day knights would come along, and the sight of them fired the king's spirit. He would have forgotten himself for sure, so I always got him well out of the road in time. He would just look with his proud eyes flashing.

On the third day, I stubbed my toe and fell. I got up softly and carefully and unstrapped my knapsack. I had a dynamite bomb in it, done up in wool. It was a good thing to have along, but it made me nervous. I got it out and just then up came a couple of knights. The king stood proudly. He'd forgotten himself again and only got to the side of the road in time.

The knights paid no attention to the king. It was his place to look out for himself.

The king was in a fury and shouted out a

A Dynamite Bomb—Just in Case!

challenge and an insult. The knights were some distance away, but halted, greatly surprised. Then they turned and started for us.

There was not a moment to lose. I flung a hair-raising, soul-scorching insult and scrambled up a great rock at the roadside.

When they were within fifteen yards, I threw the bomb, and it struck the ground under the horses' noses and blew them all to bits.

Yes, it was a neat thing. It resembled a steamboat explosion on the Mississippi. I explained it to the king as a miracle so rare it required the right weather conditions. This was in case the king wanted a repeat. For I didn't have any more bombs along.

A Rare Miracle

No Life About the Hut

Chapter 19
The Tragedy of the Manor House

On the morning of the fourth day, I decided that the king must be drilled. Otherwise we would never be able to enter any hut. I showed him how to walk with chin low and eyes to the ground. I made him take the knapsack, but his shoulders would not seem to stoop with any naturalness.

I decided to try him out, and we approached a hut but saw no life about it. The stillness was awful, like the stillness of death. The king knocked. There was no answer. I pushed the door and looked in. I made out some forms on the ground.

"Have mercy. All is taken." It was a woman's pleading voice.

"I have not come to take anything, poor woman," I replied. "I am a stranger."

"Oh, then for the fear of God, fly. This place is under the Church's curse. Go, before someone sees you and reports it."

The king had entered and was opening the shutters to let in air and light. When the light flooded her face I saw it: Smallpox!

I sprang to the king and said in his ear, "Out of the door quickly, sire, for this woman is dying of the dread disease." He did not budge.

"You mean well, but I will not go," he said. It was a desperate place for him to be in, but his mind would not be changed.

I offered the woman food and water, but she refused both. "Fair sir, my husband and daughters sleep the sleep of the dead. I shall

Smallpox!

join them soon, and I will allow nothing to come between me and death." I begged her to tell the story of how they had all come to this. So she told us.

"Years ago the lord of the manor planted fruit trees on our farm. It was ours by lease, so he could do with it what he pleased. Some time ago, three of those trees were found cut down. Our three grown sons ran to report the crime. In his lordship's dungeons they lie. We were not able to harvest our crops, nor the master's either. For this we were fined. The worst came when I cursed the Church. Since that day we are avoided. We all fell sick. There was no one who would help. Yesterday my strength broke down, and I too wait for death to free me."

By midnight it was all over. They were all dead. We covered them with rags and started away. We had not moved four steps when we heard footsteps, then a soft knock.

The Woman Tells Her Story.

"Mother, father, we have got free. Open— mother, father—"

It was the sons. Neither of us wanted to think what would happen when they pushed open the door, so we both started running as soon as we were sure we were out of hearing.

Something caught our eye as we reached the top of a hill—a red glow off in the distance.

"That's a fire," I said. We stood there awhile, looking toward the red blur and trying to make out the meaning of a faraway murmur which swelled and faded.

As we neared the fire, the murmur became a roar—a roar of men's voices. We saw a man flying by with others chasing him. This happened over and over.

A turn in the road brought us in sight of the fire. It was a large manor house, but little or nothing was left of it. By the light of the fire we saw men and women being

The Sons Return.

hunted down by the mob. Several bodies hung from trees. I warned the king this was not a safe place, so we hid, and at dawn we hurried away.

We stopped at the hut of a charcoal burner and asked for lodging. We slept till late afternoon and then joined the laborer and his wife for soup and black bread.

They told us the story of the burning manor house. Three prisoners—the three sons we had seen at the hut—had escaped and murdered the baron. The lord's servants swore revenge and activated the mob. The man and woman looked uneasy when we said we had seen the escaped prisoners the night before.

I pulled the man outside and said, "These men were related to you, weren't they?"

He turned white and said, trembling, "Ah, my God, how did you know? Poor lads. And good lads they were."

Hank Pulls the Man Outside.

"Well," I said, "they've done a righteous deed. The old baron got what he deserved. If I had my way, that would happen to all his kind." He looked at me in disbelief.

"Where are you from, that you speak so, and do not seem afraid?" he said in a cautious voice. But suddenly he became alive. "Even if you're a spy and these words are my undoing, I will have my say. I helped hang my neighbors because it would have been dangerous not to come to the lord's cause. The others helped for the same reason. But everyone secretly rejoices today that he is dead. I have said the words and feel good for it, too."

There was still hope for a republic when there was spirit such as this. This was my greatest dream. I felt I would not have to give it up for a while.

Hope for a Republic

Introducing Dowley, the Blacksmith

Chapter 20
The Yankee and the King Hold a Banquet

The coal burner's name was Marco. I asked Marco if we might visit the little hamlet. I met various people and was able to ask as many questions as I wanted to. I was pleased to see that many coins from my new money system were in use.

I got to meet several tradesmen. The most interesting fellow among them was Dowley, the blacksmith. He was doing a very good business and was highly respected. Marco was very proud of having him for a friend.

He reminded me of the splendid fellows I

had under me at the arms factory. I invited him to come out to Marco's on Sunday and dine with us. Marco was joyful for a moment. Then he grew sad. When he heard me ask the mason and the wheelwright, he turned white. I knew what the matter was. It was the cost.

So I said, "You must allow me to have these friends, and you must allow me to pay." He started to interrupt, but I said:

"Let's understand one another. I manage Jones' farm—he's the fellow back there at the house—and I am not poor. I could have a dozen feasts like this one and never care *that* for the expense." I snapped my fingers. "So you must let me pay for it all. You have opened your house to Jones and me in the most generous way."

We went about the village pricing goods and gossiping. I found a store that had everything I wanted, and I sent Marco off because

Going About the Village

I wanted everything to be a surprise.

I wrote down a list of things I wanted and handed it to the shopkeeper. He remarked that it was a pretty heavy bill. I told him not to worry, just to send the bill at dinner time Sunday.

When the things I bought arrived on Saturday afternoon, the Marcos seemed ready to faint. There was food for the dinner, but there were extras too: a dinner table, two pounds of salt, dishes, stools and so on. I told the Marcos to keep quiet about all this in front of the guests so I could show off a little. Showing off is my fatal weakness, and it was my downfall here.

Sunday was a beautiful day. Toward noon the guests arrived, and soon we were all talking like old friends. Even the king was friendly, although he was having trouble getting used to the name Jones. I asked him to try not to forget he was a farmer, but not to

Wonderful Surprises

say any more than that, for fear of giving himself away.

Dowley knew how to talk. He had begun life with nothing, but had been apprenticed to a blacksmith. His master was a fine and prosperous man, and Dowley married his daughter and took over the business.

Dowley bragged that he had fresh meat two times a month and white bread, true wheat bread, every Sunday of the year. The Dowleys had five stools, although there were only three in the family, and goblets and wooden platters. He looked at the king and me.

"Now you know what kind of man I am," he said, beaming with satisfaction.

Then Marco's wife brought out the new table. It caused quite a stir. Then she brought out two fine new stools. That was a sensation! She brought out two more, and then two more.

The New Table Causes a Stir.

The surprises piled up. Everyone gasped "oh" and "ah" as she fetched dishes and new goblets, beer, fish, chicken, a goose, eggs, roast beef, roast mutton, a ham, and lots of genuine white bread. They had never seen anything like it before.

While they sat there, the shopkeeper's son came to collect. I had him read off the items. When he finished there was an awed silence.

"Give me the grand total," I said easily, and then tossed four dollars onto the table. You should have seen them stare. "And keep the change," I said.

There was an amazed murmur. "Truly, this man is made of money. He throws it away as if it were dirt."

The clerk took the money, but could barely walk with all that wealth. I turned to the others and said calmly, "Well, the dinner is ready. Are we?"

The situation had the effect I wanted. The

"And Keep the Change."

blacksmith was simply crushed. Here he had been bragging about his meals with meat and white bread, which cost him no more than sixty cents for the year. And I had paid *four dollars* for one feast and acted like it made me tired to handle such small sums. Yes, Dowley was put in his place.

I had Dowley's respect because he thought I was prosperous and rich. We enjoyed our dinner. The king went off to take a nap. Talk drifted to business and wages.

They had fixed wages in this region. The wage was set by a magistrate or the courts, and the workers were paid that wage—no more, no less.

In fact, it was against the law to pay more. So when Dowley said that sometimes he paid more in busy times, I thought I would make a point. And when I decide to do something, I never do it halfway.

So I started out. "My friends, I can tell

Dowley Is Put in His Place.

what things will be like in the future."

"You can?" they breathed.

I told them that in the future the time would come when a man would be his own property and would be able to work where he wanted and for as long as he wanted. I told them that laws which were unfair would be changed.

"Change the laws?" they murmured. "Oh, no."

"Yes," I said. "For example, I think this law is unfair. The magistrate has fixed your wages at one cent a day. The law says that anyone who pays more shall be fined and put in the pillory. And anyone who knows and doesn't tell shall also be fined and put in the pillory. Now, Dowley, you just confessed that you have paid over the fixed wage when you needed someone to work for you!" I knew I had him.

Everyone stopped dead. I knew then I had

Hank Talks About the Future.

overdone it. I, a stranger, knew something that could send them all to the pillory, which is a terrible punishment. They were scared to death. They wanted to appeal to me, but they didn't dare.

I was nervous. I had to make us all friends again. Right now we were in danger.

Just then the king joined us from his nap, and he began to talk about farming—just what I had told him *not* to do! Cold sweat broke out all over me. I wanted to whisper in his ear, "We are in awful danger. We must win back the trust of these men." But I couldn't do it. It would look as if we were plotting.

So I had to sit and listen to him. Everything he said was wrong! He talked about growing onions in trees and digging apples from the ground.

With a glow in his eye, one of the men muttered, "Everything he says is wrong! God

In Awful Danger

has cursed the mind of this farmer!"

They rose and went for him, shouting, "You are mad, and your partner wants to betray us! Kill them! Kill them!"

Joy flamed in the king's eyes. This kind of thing was just in his line. He had been longing for a fight.

He hit the blacksmith and gave the wheelwright a crack on the jaw while I took care of the mason. Then I realized Marco was not there. He and his wife had gone for help. So I told the king we better run while we could, and I would explain things to him later.

A Fight!

Crossing the Stream

Chapter 21
The Yankee and the King Are Sold as Slaves

As we darted into the wood, I glanced back and saw a mob of excited peasants with Marco at their head. We were soon deep into the forest.

We found a stream and jumped into it. Soon we came across an oak tree with a great bough sticking out over the water. We climbed up and hid ourselves in the tree. But soon we heard the sound of the mob again. They had struck our trail and were coming down both sides of the stream. Their noise faded as they passed by underneath us.

"They will still search," said the king. "We better stay here." He was right. The noise approached again, drawing nearer and nearer. A voice from under our tree said:

"See yon tree with the overhanging branch. We would do well to send a man up it." We remained still while a peasant struggled up. The king stood up and gave the man's head a push with his foot. Down he went with a thud. The mob swarmed in.

They sent a couple men up, but the king kicked them all down. We thought we had them beaten until we began to smell smoke! They had built a fire under our tree. A thick cloud began to roll up the tree. There was nothing we could do. Coughing, we made our way down. We traded blows thick and fast when suddenly some horsemen tore into the crowd and a voice shouted:

"Hold—or you are dead men!"

How good it sounded! The owner of the

Smoke!

voice was a gentleman. The mob fell back as he said to them, "What are ye doing to these people?"

"They are madmen, sir, and have come—"

"Peace," he said. "Ye know not what you say. They are not mad. Who are you? Explain."

"We are but peaceful strangers, sir," I said, "and from a far country. We mean no harm. We are not mad, nor violent either."

The gentleman sent the peasants away and continued to question us. We revealed nothing other than we were strangers from a far country. We were then mounted on some of the gentleman's horses, and we rode with the party to a roadside inn.

At dawn, we made ready to start. The lord's chief attendant came forward and said, "My lord commands that you ride with us to the town of Cambenet. There you will be out of danger."

Saved by a Gentleman

We had no choice but to ride, and we arrived at the market square in the forenoon.

A crowd had gathered around a poor band of slaves. I lingered, full of pity when—Click! The king and I were handcuffed together. Our companions, the servants, had done it. The gentleman stood looking on. The king burst out in a fury:

"What is the meaning of this joke?"

The gentleman merely said, "Put up the slaves and sell them."

Slaves! The word had a new sound—and how unspeakably awful!

We loudly proclaimed ourselves freemen. Someone from the crowd shouted, "If indeed ye are freemen, then prove it!" The king stormed:

"You're insane! This scoundrel should prove that we are *not* freemen."

The leader said only, "Ye are strangers to us. Ye may be freemen, but ye may also be

Slaves!

slaves. You must prove that you are not."

"Dear sir," I interrupted, "give us time to send to the Valley of Holiness—"

"That is an unusual request, and you may not hope to have it granted," he said.

So we were sold at auction. In a big town with an active market, we should have brought a good price. This place was out of the way, and I am ashamed every time I think of the price we brought. The King of England brought seven dollars and I brought nine.

So we became the rear end of the slave procession and marched out of town at noon. We passed all manner of people, and no one for the world would have recognized King Arthur and his chief minister.

Sold at Auction

In the Slave Procession

Chapter 22
The Fight in the Dark

The king brooded. This was natural. But he did not brood about his sudden fall from the highest place in the world to the lowest. No! He brooded about the price he had brought! He couldn't get over the seven dollars. In order to quiet his constant protests, I told him that he ought to have brought twenty-five dollars. But I knew the world had never seen a king that was worth half the money.

The slave driver saw right away that no one would purchase the king on account of his style. No one wanted a slave like that! I could have told our owner that I had a difficult job reducing the king's style to a peasant's style. But to reduce it to a slave's style—that would be a large task.

He lashed and clubbed and beat the king until his body was a sight to see, but Arthur's spirit remained untouched. Even the slave driver could see that there was such a thing as a slave whose manhood he could not break.

We had a rough time tramping to and fro. All the while I wanted to get free, but I was not willing to take desperate chances. But I became ready and willing to take a chance after I heard the king say that when he got free he would abolish slavery.

I set about a plan. It would require time and patience, but it would have a great effect. My idea was to get loose some night, along with the king, then gag and bind our master, change clothes with him, hitch him

Nothing Can Break Arthur's Spirit.

to the slave chain, and march to Camelot.

The plan would work only if I could get hold of a thin piece of iron which I could shape into a lockpick. I could then undo the locks that held our chains.

My chance came at last. A gentleman had come twice before to look at me. I never expected to belong to him, but he had something which I wanted. It was a long steel pin, which he used to fasten together his outside garment. There were three of these pins, and the third time he came around, he came close enough to me so that I could grab one.

I was glad for a moment, then sad. I heard the slave owner and the gentleman settling on a price for the king and me. He said he would come for us tomorrow. If we were to escape, it had to be tonight.

I whispered in the king's ear:

"Tonight we shall both be free. With this thing I have stolen, I will unlock these locks

Hank Grabs One of the Pins.

and cast off these chains. When the slave owner comes about nine-thirty to inspect us for the night, we will grab him, gag him, beat him, and early in the morning we'll march out of this town."

That evening we waited patiently for our fellow slaves to fall asleep. I had to work carefully so as not to cause a rattle. Finally I got my last iron off. I breathed relief and reached for the king's irons. Too late! The master came in with a light in his hand. I kept a sharp lookout and prepared to spring on him the moment he bent over me.

But he didn't approach. He stopped, set down his light, and went out the door.

"Quick!" said the king. "Bring him back!"

I was up in a minute and raced out into the dark night. I saw a dim figure a few steps away and threw myself upon it. We fought and drew a crowd. Then lanterns appeared. They belonged to the night watchmen, who

The Master Comes with a Light.

were coming to see what the disturbance was.

Presently I felt hands on my shoulders, and both of us were marched off to prison. Here was disaster! I tried to imagine what would happen when the master discovered it was I he had been fighting with.

Just then he turned his face in my direction, and it caught the light. By George, he was the wrong man!

Watchmen Come Running!

The Court Believes Hank.

Chapter 23
An Awful Situation

I was taken to prison, and there I spent a sleepless night, wondering what had happened over at the slave quarters.

When morning came at last, I was brought to court. I gave this explanation. I said I was a slave of an earl who was taken ill just outside the city. I had been ordered to find and bring back the best doctor in the city when this common man had jumped me and started beating me in the night.

The common man interrupted and started to say that it was I who had rushed upon him. But the court believed me. They begged my pardon and hoped the lordship had not suffered because of my imprisonment.

I took my leave and rushed to the slave quarters. Empty! Everybody gone! Everybody except for one—the slave master. His body had been battered to a pulp. The place looked like there had been a terrible fight.

I found a man who told me the story.

"There were sixteen slaves here," he said, "who rose against their master in the night. The slave who was most valuable got free of his bonds by magic, and when the master discovered his loss, he threw himself on the other slaves. They broke his neck and beat him until he was dead."

"Dreadful," I said. "What will happen at the trial?"

"The trial is over and they are all condemned to die within twenty-four hours. But they may wait until they find the missing

Everybody Gone!

one and then hang them all. They are searching for him everywhere and will probably find him before nightfall."

The missing one! It made me feel awful!

I needed a disguise. At the first second-hand clothing store, I found a seaman's outfit and bound my face with a bandage to cover the worst bruises.

I found the telegraphic wire and followed it to the office. The young fellow in charge was sleeping when I burst in.

"Quick now!" I said. "Call Camelot. I am a desperate man!"

"What?" he asked. "How does one such as you know about this tele—"

I interrupted. "Stop gabbling. Call the palace." He made the call. "Now ask for Clarence," I ordered. We waited five minutes—how long it seemed!—and then came a click and Clarence's voice.

"Now then," I said, "the king is here and in

Bursting into the Telegraph Office

danger. We were captured and brought here as slaves, and we need help. Send five hundred knights with Launcelot as fast as you can. Tell them to enter by the south gate and look for a man with a white cloth around his right arm."

His answer was prompt. "They shall start in half an hour."

I immediately started figuring. Knights and horses in heavy armor couldn't travel very fast. They would arrive at six. But it would still be light enough for them to see the white cloth.

I left to go out and buy a new disguise, but once on the street, I ran right into one of our slaves. He and a guard were looking for me. The slave gave me a look that went right through me. I ducked into a shop and edged my way to the back to escape out the rear door. But as I stepped out into the back alley, the officer cut me off. I walked right into his handcuffs.

Walking into the Handcuffs

I asked the slave why he had betrayed me, and he said with surprise, "What, would I let you, of all men, escape and not hang with us when you're the cause of our death?"

"You're not going to be hanged. None of us are," I said.

Both men laughed. "Oh yes you are," said the guard. "And now, since you, the missing slave, have been found, you will all hang *today* at midafternoon!"

Oh, that shot hit home! My knights would not be able to arrive in time. They would be three hours too late. Nothing in the world could save me and the King of England.

"You Will All Hang Today!"

The Hanging

Chapter 24
Sir Launcelot and the Knights
to the Rescue

It was four in the afternoon and there we all sat on our tall scaffold. Huge crowds had gathered to see the hanging. I still had the bandage, just in case. Presently the Sheriff of London called for silence. He read out our crime. A priest said a prayer.

Then the first slave was blindfolded, and the rope was pulled. A noose was placed on the second slave. Then the third was hung. It was dreadful. I turned my head away. When I turned back I missed the king! They were blindfolding him! I couldn't move. I was choking. They finished blindfolding him and led him under the rope. But when they put the rope around his neck, I jumped to his rescue. And what should I see then but five hundred knights on bicycles coming down the road.

I waved my right arm at Launcelot. He recognized the white rag and shouted, "On your knees, everyone, and salute the king!"

The astonished crowd went down to their knees and begged the king, whom they had been about to hang, for forgiveness. The king received their homage in his rags.

And then up came Clarence. He winked at me and said, "Good surprise, wasn't it? I've had the knights practicing on their bicycles for a long time. And they were just hungry for a chance to show off!"

Five Hundred Knights on Bicycles

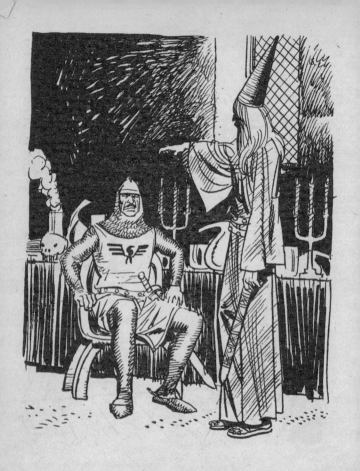

Merlin Has Been Busy.

Chapter 25
The Yankee's Fight
with the Knights

Home again, at Camelot. The date was set for my combat with Sir Sagramour. No one talked of anything else. For the whole nation knew that this was not going to be a duel between two knights. No, it was going to be a duel between the two mighty magicians, Merlin and me. Merlin had been busy lately giving Sir Sagramour supernatural powers.

But to me, there was a greater matter at stake. I was entering the tournaments to achieve a long-sought goal. I was out to destroy knight-errantry. The knights considered themselves to be a special class of men. And as long as their order existed, there would be no equality among men.

There were no vacant seats on the day of the tournament. The grandstand was clothed with flags, streamers and rich tapestries. All the royalty were there in silks and velvets. The knights were there too, waiting for their chance. My feeling toward their order was not much of a secret, and they all had come to defend knight-errantry. By the rules, if I won my fight with Sir Sagramour, others had the right to challenge me.

At the appointed hour, the king made a sign. There was a bugle blast. Out from his tent rode Sir Sagramour on his horse, both dressed in heavy armor and rich trappings.

Then I came out. I was in a gymnast's costume. I wore flesh-colored tights from neck to heel and blue silk shorts. My horse, who was small and light, wore only a cowboy saddle. Everyone gasped.

In a Gymnast's Uniform

Sir Sagramour and I saluted each other and then bowed to the king and queen. We each rode to our sides. Old Merlin stepped forward and threw some magic threads over Sir Sagramour.

The bugles blew. Sir Sagramour came thundering down the course. When his lance point was two yards from my chest, I twitched my horse aside. The big knight swept by. There was applause for me. We did this several times more, and then Sagramour lost his temper and started chasing me down. But I was lighter and swifter, and he soon gave that up and went back to his side to come again. This time he came in earnest.

I slipped my lasso from the horn of my saddle and sat on my horse with ease. I swung my lasso in wide circles about my head as he started down the course. When there were forty feet between us, I sent the lasso out around him and pulled it tight. Sir

The Lasso Lands Around Sagramour.

Sagramour was pulled out of his saddle! It was a sensation! These people had never seen any cowboy tricks before and they shouted with delight.

Another knight was up and ready as soon as my lasso was released and Sir Sagramour had been helped to his tent. Here he came. I dodged. He passed and my lasso fell around him. A second later, fst! His saddle was empty.

I got another and another. When I had lassoed five, the knights stopped. Then they decided to send their finest and greatest knights against me. I lassoed them. They decided to bring out the mightiest of the mighty—Sir Launcelot himself.

The lasso went spinning through the air, and before you could wink, I was towing Sir Launcelot across the field on his back. Thunderous applause greeted me!

I coiled my lasso and hung it on my saddle

Towing the Mighty Launcelot

horn. Closing my eyes, I said to myself, "No one will fight me. Knight-errantry is dead." I was so sure that I was astonished to hear the bugle announce another challenger. I looked down and saw that my lasso was gone. Only then did I notice Merlin slipping away. He had stolen it!

It was Sir Sagramour again. This time he was going to fight with his sword. I would never be able to dodge his mighty sword. We rode forward to salute the royalty.

"Where is your strange weapon?" asked the king. He was worried for me.

"It is stolen, sire," I answered.

"Do you have another?"

Again I answered, "No, sire, I brought only one."

Other knights offered me their swords, but I said I would fight with my own weapons.

So we rode to our stations. The king finally gave the signal. Sir Sagramour came, his

The Lasso Is Gone!

long. sword flashing. I sat still. On he came. The people shouted at me to fly, but I did not budge until he was fifteen steps from me.

Then I snatched a revolver out of my holster. There was a flash and a roar. The revolver was back in its holster before anyone knew what had happened.

Sir Sagramour's horse plunged by, its saddle empty. Sir Sagramour lay stone dead.

The people who ran to him were amazed to find him dead, and no reason for it except a tiny hole in his armor. They attached no importance to a little thing like that.

I was requested to come and explain the miracle. Instead I said:

"If anyone doubts that this combat was fairly won, I do not wait for them to challenge me. I challenge them. I challenge all! Here I stand, and dare the knights of England to come against me—not one by one, but all together! Take my challenge, or I will

Hank's New Weapon—A Revolver

proclaim you all defeated!"

It was a bluff. But in no time, five hundred knights sprang into their saddles and started coming for me. I grabbed a revolver in each hand.

Bang! One saddle empty. Bang! Another one. Bang—Bang! Two down. But I knew I had only eleven bullets in my two guns.

When the ninth man fell, I saw a wavering. I raised both revolvers and pointed them. The knights stood their ground one instant, and then broke and fled.

The day was mine. Knight-errantry was doomed. The march of civilization could begin.

Knight-Errantry Falls.

The Challenge Engraved in Brass

Chapter 26
Three Years Later

Since I had conquered knight-errantry, I no longer felt I had to work in secret. The very next day I showed my hidden schools, factories and workshops.

I renewed my challenge. I had it engraved on brass and posted where any priest could read it. And during the next three years the knights gave me no trouble.

Over these three years, England was becoming prosperous and happy. Schools were everywhere. Slavery was gone. All men were equal before the law. We had the telephone, telegraph, phonograph and typewriter, and electricity and railroads too.

All the knights were put into useful employment. Because of their experience in wandering, I used them to spread our civilization all over the land.

But I had two schemes which were the grandest of all my projects. The first was to take away the power of the Church. The other project was to set up a republic after Arthur's death, where all men and women would be given the right to vote.

As for me, I married Sandy. And she was a prize. She had hunted all over England for me and had found me after the slave hanging in London. She resumed her place at my side, and so we decided to have a wedding. We had a child, a little girl, who was the joy of our lives. I was happy. Things were moving along.

This was the situation when the little one

Hank and Sandy Have a Child.

was taken ill. I dropped everything, and Sandy and I stood watch for three days and nights till the child was out of danger.

The doctors said we must take the child away to coax her back to health. She must have sea air, they said.

So we took a ship and cruised. Tiring of this after two weeks, we stepped ashore on the French coast to rest for a while.

At the end of a month I sent the ship home for fresh supplies and news. We expected it back in three or four days.

Again the child began to lose ground. Again Sandy and I stood watch, day in and day out. She was so sick we wouldn't allow anyone to help. For two and a half weeks we watched by the crib and forgot the world outside.

At last the child began to get well. It was then we both realized that more than two weeks had passed and the ship was not back

Watching by the Crib

yet!

I rode to a hilltop overlooking the sea. Not a sail in sight. I told Sandy this awful news. There must be an explanation. An earthquake? An invasion? A plague?

I decided to go and borrowed a ship. I approached England the next morning. There were ships in the harbor at Dover, but there was no sign of life about them.

It was Sunday, but there was not a priest in sight. No bells tolled. The streets were strangely quiet and empty.

I passed a church. There in the belfry was the bell, but it was covered with a black cloth. Then I understood. It was worse than an invasion. It was the INTERDICT! The Interdict was the Church's most severe punishment. The whole nation lay under its curse. No one could be blessed. All churches were locked.

What had happened to have caused this? I

The Interdict!

had to get to Camelot.

It was a miserable journey. The whole country was silent. Men did not talk or laugh. The London Tower showed signs of war. Much had happened while I was gone.

I arrived in Camelot late in the night. It was completely dark. I found no life stirring in the streets. The vast castle loomed black on the hilltop. There wasn't a light in sight. So this was what the Church wanted—to snuff out all my beautiful civilization just like that.

The drawbridge was down. The great gate stood wide. My footsteps were the only sound I heard as I entered those huge, empty courts.

An Empty Courtyard

Alone and Sad

Chapter 27
War!

I found Clarence alone and sad. In place of electric light, he had an ancient rag lamp. He sprang up when he saw me saying, "Oh, it's so good to look upon a live person!"

Before he could say anything else, I said, "Quick, now, tell me the meaning of this disaster. How did it come about?"

"It would have happened by and by," he sighed. "But it was the queen's fault. The queen and Sir Launcelot. They were in love. But King Arthur hated to believe it.

"Two of the king's evil nephews, Mordred

and Agravaine, decided to call the king's attention to the queen's love of Launcelot. A trap was laid and Launcelot walked into it. War between the king and Launcelot was the result, with some knights siding with the king and others with Launcelot.

"The king sent Guenever to the stake. But Launcelot and his knights rescued her, killing many of our old friends.

"The rest of the tale is just war, pure and simple. Launcelot retreated to his castle, and the king followed. The Church patched up a peace between Arthur and Launcelot and the queen. But it didn't work. Arthur pursued Launcelot and left the kingdom in Mordred's hands till you should return.

"Evil Mordred set to work to make himself king. He was going to marry Guenever, but she shut herself up in the Tower of London. Mordred attacked. Then the Church proclaimed the Interdict.

Launcelot Rescued Guenever.

"The knights urged the king to stop the battles. But King Arthur swore he would not stop until he killed the traitor, Mordred. Arthur did kill Mordred. But before Mordred died, he dealt Arthur a death blow. And poor soul, he is dead."

I was stunned. "And the queen?"

"She is a nun" was his answer.

"What changes! I cannot believe it!" I cried. "What next, I wonder?"

"I can tell you," Clarence answered grimly. "The Church is master now. You were mentioned in the Interdict along with Mordred. It is not to be removed while you remain alive. The Church has gathered all the knights that are left alive to fight you."

"But we have our schools, our workshops, our—"

"Save your breath! We have under sixty men, boys—I mean. When the knights come, all our people will go over to the enemy. You

A Death Blow

see, they still have all their old fears.

"But," he continued, "I have prepared for the worst. I'll tell you what I've done, and why. Smart as you are, the Church is smarter. It was the Church that sent you away. The doctors who told you to go were servants of the Church."

"Clarence!" I exclaimed.

"It is true," he said. "And every person on the ship was a servant of the Church too. When the ship returned, the captain told me you were sailing for Spain. I grew troubled. I had heard no word from you, and I knew you would have informed me. I was going to send a ship for you. But our navy suddenly disappeared. The railway, telephone and telegraph also suddenly stopped. All the poles were cut down. The Church laid a ban on the electric light!

"I knew I had to act! From our factories I selected fifty-two faithful boys. All have been

Troubled by the Captain's News

in training for over ten years. But they are young enough so they do not fear the Church's terrors.

"I visited Merlin's cave, where we had set up our great electric plant so many years ago. I have readied it for a battle.

"We took wire fencing and put up ten wire fences around the entrance to the cave. The fences are charged with electricity with wires that go from the inside of the cave out to the ten circles. So that when any man or beast touches it, he will be electrocuted.

"I've placed guns and ammunition at every approach and built a gunning platform at the entrance. Dynamite mines have been placed under the ground around the outer fence. If anyone steps on them, they will explode."

I sat and thought awhile. "Yes, everything is ready. We must rise up and strike now. We'll proclaim a republic! That will start

Ten Wire Fences

things off." I dictated:

BE IT KNOWN. THE KING HAS DIED AND LEFT NO HEIR. BY THE POWER VESTED IN ME, A REPUBLIC IS HEREBY PROCLAIMED. ALL MEN ARE NOW EQUAL!

I signed it "the Boss."

"We'll print it and post it and grab a bicycle, and off for Merlin's cave! It's a pleasant palace. I wonder if we shall ever see it again," I said as we left.

Off for Merlin's Cave!

Turning His Diary into This Book

Chapter 28
The Last Battle

IN MERLIN'S CAVE—It was Clarence and I and fifty-two bright, well-educated boys who saw the last battle. We waited in the cave a week. During that time, I finished turning my diary into this book.

I had spies out, of course. And what we had expected was happening. The nation cheered for the republic for one day and then turned around and joined the Church and the nobles. The knights led the way, thirty thousand strong. These were all the knights who remained after the war.

At dawn on the big day the sentry reported that the host of knights was moving slowly toward us. The front ranks were on horses. There was the sound of bugles and they broke into a gallop. Nearer, nearer, they came to us, but then they hit the dynamite mines. Everything exploded with a thunder-crash, and five thousand were blown into the sky.

All along the ground lay a thick wall of smoke on the outside of our circles of wire. When it lifted, we saw that the dynamite mines had dug a ditch more than a hundred feet wide on the outside of the last fence. No life was in sight.

I sent a few lookouts up on the embankment that had been thrown up. By nightfall the sentries reported that a few knights were making their way toward us. But they didn't have a chance.

I tested all the electric signals—the ones on

The Dynamite Mines Explode!

the gun platform and the ones which shot power through the fences. Each fence had its own electric current and could work independently of the others.

I knew what the knights would do. I told Clarence that under cover of night, they would quietly fill the great ditch made by the dynamite blast and then try to swarm over the embankment at dawn.

I turned on the current of the two inner fences. The other eight fences I left without current until later.

Clarence and I then crept out and lay down between the two inside fences. Clarence suddenly said, "What is that?"

"What is what?" I asked.

We gazed toward a dark shape. It looked like a man leaning against the fence. We crept toward it until we were pretty close. Yes, it was a man kneeling with both hands on the upper wire—dead as he could be. He

A Man Leaning Against the Fence

had touched the charged wires. And he never knew what hit him.

We made out another knight approaching. He stood a moment, wondering why the other one didn't move. As he moved forward, he too touched the wire and uttered a soft moan as he sank down. Other knights came, bringing only their swords. Every now and then we would see a blue spark as a knight touched the fence. Everywhere dead men were lying outside the second fence. It was clear that our current was so strong it killed before the victim could cry out.

Then we heard a muffled sound. It was the army coming. But they got no further than the second fence. We could make out a dark mass of dead men piling up on the outside of the second fence. We were being closed in by a wall of dead men!

We returned to the cave and I sent a current through the third fence, then the fourth

Strong Current

and the fifth. Next, I pressed a button and on came fifty huge spotlights. The sudden glare stopped the army for a moment. During that moment I sent current through all the fences and struck the whole army dead in their tracks.

The rest of the knights were between us and the great ditch. I then let a great stream of water I had held back come rushing through the ditch. It created a huge roar. We opened fire with our guns, and those who were not shot jumped over the embankment and were drowned in the river.

We had won. We were masters of England. Twenty-five thousand lay dead around us.

Twenty-Five Thousand Dead

A Knight Stabs the Boss.

Chapter 29
Clarence Writes the End

I, Clarence, must write the end.

The Boss proposed that we go out to help any wounded. I told him it was not wise but he insisted. We turned off the current and moved out to the field.

The Boss went up to the first wounded man we heard asking for help. The knight recognized him and stabbed him.

We carried the Boss back to the cave and gave his wound the best care we could.

A few days after the Boss was hurt, a simple peasant goodwife appeared and offered to cook for us, saying her people had gone off. We did not know that this was really Merlin, who had disguised himself as an old woman.

We were glad to have this woman, for we were short of hands.

You see, we were in a trap. Only in our cave were we safe. Once we left it, we were no longer protected.

But a terrible thing was happening. The dead bodies of the twenty-five thousand knights we had killed started giving off poisonous fumes. These fumes were killing us off. It was difficult for us to leave. But we would have to, or we'd die. We had won the battle, but in a way, we really had not. We were trapped.

One night I awoke at midnight and saw the woman making curious passes in the air over the Boss's head. Everyone was asleep. The woman started tiptoeing toward the door. "Stop!" I called out. "What have you been doing?"

Clarence Stops "the Woman."

She halted and screamed:

"You were conquerers but you are conquered. You all shall die in this place—except *him*. He sleeps now—and shall sleep thirteen centuries. I am Merlin!"

He started laughing horribly and couldn't stop. He rolled around the ground until finally he came up against one of our charged wires and was killed. But his face was fixed in that horrible grin.

The Boss has not stirred. He sleeps like stone. If he does not wake, we will hide his body in the deepest place in the cave. We will leave him this manuscript, and then we will try to leave.

"He Shall Sleep Thirteen Centuries!"

ILLUSTRATED CLASSIC EDITIONS

ILLUSTRATED CLASSIC EDITIONS

MOBY BOOKS